Rock Star

Felice Arena and Phil Kettle

illustrated by
Gus Gordon

First published in Great Britain by
RISING STARS UK LTD 2004
76 Farnaby Road, Bromley, BR1 4BH

Reprinted 2004, 2005

For information visit our website at:
www.risingstars-uk.com

British Library Cataloguing in Publication Data

A CIP record for this book is available from the British Library.

ISBN: 1-904591-79-5

First published in 2003 by
MACMILLAN EDUCATION AUSTRALIA PTY LTD
627 Chapel Street, South Yarra, Australia 3141

Associated companies and representatives throughout the world.

Copyright © Felice Arena and Phil Kettle 2003

Project Management by Limelight Press Pty Ltd
Cover and text design by Lore Foye
Illustrations by Gus Gordon

Printed and bound in Great Britain by
Mackays of Chatham plc, Chatham, Kent

Contents

Billy   Sam

CHAPTER 1

Oh When the Saints ...

Best friends Sam and Billy are
hanging out together in Sam's
garage. Sam has recently taken up
guitar lessons and is showing off
what he's learned to Billy on his
brand new electric guitar.

Sam "I can only play two songs so far—'Row, Row, Row Your Boat' and 'When the Saints Go Marching In'."

Billy "Cool. Play 'em."

Sam "Okay."

Sam carefully places his fingers on the correct starting chord position.

Sam (strumming) "This is chord D."

Billy "Good."

Sam (more strumming) "And this is chord G."

Billy "Okay, I get it. Now play something."

Sam "Yeah, hang on. I'm just showing you what I know. Right, here goes ..."

Sam begins to strum continuously:
Oh, when the saints, oh, when the saints, oh, when ... Sam stops strumming. His fingers fumble to find the next chord.

Sam "... *oh, when ... the ... sai ... nts ...*"

Billy "Yeah, is that it?"

Sam "I haven't finished yet! ... *go ... mar ... ch ... ing ... in.*"

Billy "Can I have a go?"

Sam "Um ..."

Billy "Come on, I won't wreck it. I just want to see what it feels like."

CHAPTER 2

Oh Yeah!

Sam reluctantly hands over his guitar to Billy. Billy madly strums it as if he's grating cheese. He also starts to sing made-up lyrics—badly.

Billy (singing) *"Oh Yeah ... oh yeah baby ... oh yeah ... You make my heart bleed and my nose too ... yeah, yeah, yeah ..."*
Sam "What are you doing?"

Billy doesn't hear Sam. Squinting his eyes and biting his top lip, he continues to pluck the instrument, lost in his own world. Sam suddenly snatches the guitar from him.

Sam "What do you think you're doing?"

Billy "I was just playing your guitar."

Sam "No you weren't—it was gross."

Billy "It was not. That's how you're *meant* to play an electric guitar."

Sam "No way ..."

Billy "Yeah really! I've never heard of any rock legend playing 'Oh, When the Saints'! Maybe on a recorder, but never on an electric guitar."

Sam "Yeah, well I don't know if ..."

Sam stops mid-sentence realising what Billy has just said.

Sam "Rock legend? What do you mean, 'rock legend'?"

Billy "Well, if you're learning to play a really cool guitar like that, what else are you goin' to be?"

Sam "Hmm ... rock legend ... yeah, I could be a rock star!"

CHAPTER 3

Our Band

Sam thinks for a minute. The idea of being famous is really sounding good.

Sam "I've got a better idea. We can *both* be rock stars. We'll put together our own band!"

Billy "Cool. So are you goin' to play guitar?"

Sam "Yeah, and I want to be the
lead singer too, and have all the
fans fall all over me."

Billy "Really? All those girls with
their hands all over you—wow,
great choice ... not!"

Sam "Yeah, well I love to sing.
Didn't you just hear me? And I'd
just have to wear chick repellent."

Billy "Is *that* what you were doing?"

Sam "Okay, so I don't have a voice like Eminem or that big Italian opera singer Pav-lova-rotti or whatever his name is, but it doesn't matter ..."

Billy "Why?"

Sam "We can be heavy metal. The singers just scream in those bands. Doesn't matter what your voice sounds like, so you can sing too."

Billy "Yeah, I guess. Okay, cool. But we need more band members."

Sam "What about Dom to play drums? He's always getting in trouble at school for tapping his pens on his desk. And we can ask Luke to play keyboards. He already plays piano."

Billy "Good one."

Sam "Now, all we need is a really
cool name."

Sam and Billy pause for a
moment, and look around the garage
for some good band name ideas.

Billy "What about 'The Bike Chains' ... nah, that's dumb. I know, 'The Cardboard Boxes'."

Sam "You've got to be joking. It has to be tough-sounding like 'The Brick Heads', or have something to do with us."

Billy "I know, I know ..."

CHAPTER 4

The Greatest Band

Billy leaps to his feet as the best name springs into his mind.

Billy "What about 'The Nits'!"

Sam "What?"

Billy "'The Nits'. Remember how
you gave me head lice back in Year
Two?"

Sam "Oh yeah, I forgot. That was
years ago."

Billy "Well, we didn't really hang
out with each other before then. If
it wasn't for your nits jumping
onto my head we might not have
become best friends."

Sam "You're right. That's a cool name … 'The Nits'. I can see it now … 50 000 people crammed in a stadium, wearing their Nits T-shirts and screaming, 'We want The Nits! We want The Nits' …"

Billy "Yeah, and there's lights flashing all over the stage …"

Sam rushes over to the light
switch in the garage and flicks it up
and down several times.

Billy "Then we walk on stage and
the crowd goes wild. We're the
greatest band on the planet."

Sam leaves the light switch and joins Billy again.

Sam "Then I hold up my guitar and strum an awesome chord that booms through the super giant speakers and echoes right around the stadium."

Billy "And I step forward and pick up my microphone."

Billy turns and picks up one of Sam's dad's golf clubs which is leaning against the back corner of the garage. He brings the golf club up close to his mouth, pretending it's a microphone.

Billy "... and then I sing the greatest song ever!"

Sam suddenly begins strumming the chords to "When the Saints ...".

CHAPTER 5

Smash Hit

Billy and Sam pretend to be rock
stars for several more minutes. Sam
continues to play the only three
chords he knows while Billy alternates
between being a lead singer and
banging on an upside-down bucket as
the group's drummer. Their
"performance" is suddenly interrupted
when Sam's mother calls for him.

Sam "Awwh man, we were just getting into it."

Billy "This isn't good for our image. When The Nits go on tour the folks have to stay at home."

Sam "That's for sure. I'll just be a sec. *Don't* play my guitar."

Sam leaves the garage, while Billy patiently waits for him to return. Billy stares at the guitar, eager to pick it up even though Sam has strictly told him not to. Eventually Billy can't resist it any longer—he grabs the guitar and starts strumming it.

Billy "… And the crowd are no longer screaming 'We want The Nits, we want The Nits' … but it's 'We want Billy, we want Billy' …"

Billy falls to his knees, frantically strumming the guitar like a mad man. He gets carried away imagining he is a rock legend and starts swinging the guitar above his head. Like all good heavy metal guitarists, he then begins to smash the guitar on the garage ground. The instrument breaks into a thousand pieces just as Sam returns.

Sam "NO!!!!!!!!!!!!!!!!!!"

Sam suddenly springs up out of
bed, panting heavily with beads of
sweat racing down his face. He looks
over and sees that his electric guitar
is intact—safe and well, leaning by his
bedside table.

He realises that it was all a bad dream—Billy and him in the garage, The Nits, everything—just one big nightmare. Later that morning, Sam's mum calls Sam to answer the front door. It's Billy. Sam's mum suggests that Sam shows Billy his new guitar.

Billy "You got a guitar? Cool. Give us a look."

Sam "Yeah, but it's no big deal. Let's play basketball?"

Billy "Yeah, okay."

Sam "Great, let's go."

Sam smiles to himself, relieved that he isn't a rock legend—for now.

amplifier A big, black box that makes the loudest noise even louder than it was before.

drum An instrument which has a tight skin stretched over a hollow base. You beat the skin with a stick to make the loudest noise possible.

rock music Music with a constant beat that makes your hips and head shake.

singer The person in the band who tries to sing louder than the noise the drums make.

Rock Star Must-dos

☞ When practising in the garage, make sure you always keep the garage door closed—you want to keep the neighbours happy!

☞ If your neighbours do complain about the noise, ask them if they would like to join the band.

☞ Practise your groovy moves while looking in the mirror.

☞ Try to be the drummer in a band—they make the most noise and it's the best fun.

☞ If your dog howls while your band is playing, you need to practise a lot more.

☞ You can practise some air guitar with your tennis racquet.

☞ Sometimes it might be good to practise in the park but be careful not to scare the birds away.

☞ Practise signing your autograph—you never know when you might become famous.

☞ If your parents complain about the amount of noise your band makes, next time you get your pocket money, buy them some ear plugs.

BOYS RULE!
Rock Star
Instant Info

 The world's largest drum kit has 308 pieces.

 The biggest organ in the world is as loud as 25 brass bands put together.

 Michael Jackson's "Thriller" album has sold over 47 million copies since 1982—it's the biggest selling album of all time.

 There are more boy bands than there are girl bands.

 The BBC's record library has over one million records.

The first record—a gramophone record—was made in 1885.

 The first CD to sell one million copies was "Brothers in Arms" by a band called Dire Straits.

 Kylie Minogue earned five million dollars from her 2001 tour of Australia—a record (not the playing kind) for a solo Australian performer.

 Your parents love to hear you practise singing and playing musical instruments—the louder, the better!

Think Tank

1 What does the lead singer in a band do?

2 What is a duet?

3 What instrument in a rock band makes the most noise?

4 When was the first record made?

5 Is country and western music much like rock music?

6 What is an air guitar?

7 Are there more boy bands or girl bands?

8 How many band members were there in The Beatles?

Answers

1 The lead singer sings the main part of the songs and usually stands at the front.

2 A duet is when two people sing together.

3 The drums make the most noise in a rock band.

4 The first record was made in 1885.

5 Country and western music is nothing at all like rock music.

6 An air guitar is a pretend guitar you play in the air.

7 There are more boy bands than girl bands.

8 There were four band members in The Beatles.

How did you score?

- If you got 8 answers correct, then you should get your best friend and together form your own band.

- If you got 6 answers correct, maybe you should just go and listen to rock bands.

- If you got fewer than 4 answers correct, then the best you can hope to do is play some air guitar.

Felice → ← Phil

Hi Guys!
We have loads of fun reading and want
you to, too. We both believe that being a
good reader is really important and so
cool. Try out our suggestions to help you
have fun as you read.

At school, why don't you use "Rock
Star" as a play and you and your friends
can be the actors. Set the scene for your
play. What props do you need? Maybe
you could take a guitar or drum kit to
school, or just use your imagination to
pretend that you are about to go on stage
at a rock festival.

So ... have you decided who is going to
be Billy and who is going to be Sam?
Now, with your friends, read and act out
our story in front of the class.

We have a lot of fun when we go to schools and read our stories. After we finish, the kids all clap really loudly. When you've finished your play your classmates will do the same. Just remember to look out of the window—there might be a talent scout from a television station watching you!

Reading at home is really important and a lot of fun as well.

Take our books home and get someone in your family to read them with you. Maybe they can take on a part in the story.

Remember, reading is a whole lot of fun.

So, as the frog in the local pond would say, Read-it!

And remember, Boys Rule!

BOYS RULE!

When We Were Kids

Felice

Phil

Phil "You were a rock legend as a kid, weren't you?"

Felice "Yes, I performed in a rock concert in London once."

Phil "Were you any good?"

Felice "I was more than good, I was sensational!"

Phil "Why, what happened?"

Felice "I forgot the words to one of the songs."

Phil "So what did you do?"

Felice "I just went 'la la la' all the way through it, and the crowd called out for more."

Phil "Oh, just like all the great stars!"

What a Laugh!

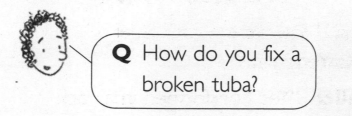

Q How do you fix a broken tuba?

A With a tuba glue.

BOYS RULE!

Gone Fishing

The Tree House

Golf Legends

Camping Out

Bike Daredevils

Water Rats

Skateboard
Dudes

Tennis Ace

Basketball
Buddies

Secret Agent
Heroes

Wet World

Rock Star

Pirate Attack

Olympic
Champions

Race Car
Dreamers

Hit the Beach

Rotten
School Day

Halloween
Gotcha!

Battle of the
Games

On the Farm

BOYS RULE! books are available from most booksellers.
For mail order information please call Rising Stars
on **01933 443862** or visit **www.risingstars-uk.com**